The Beach

Written by Alison Hawes
Illustrated by Lisa Smith

Collins

Look! We can see the seagulls.

3

Look! We can see the ice-cream van.

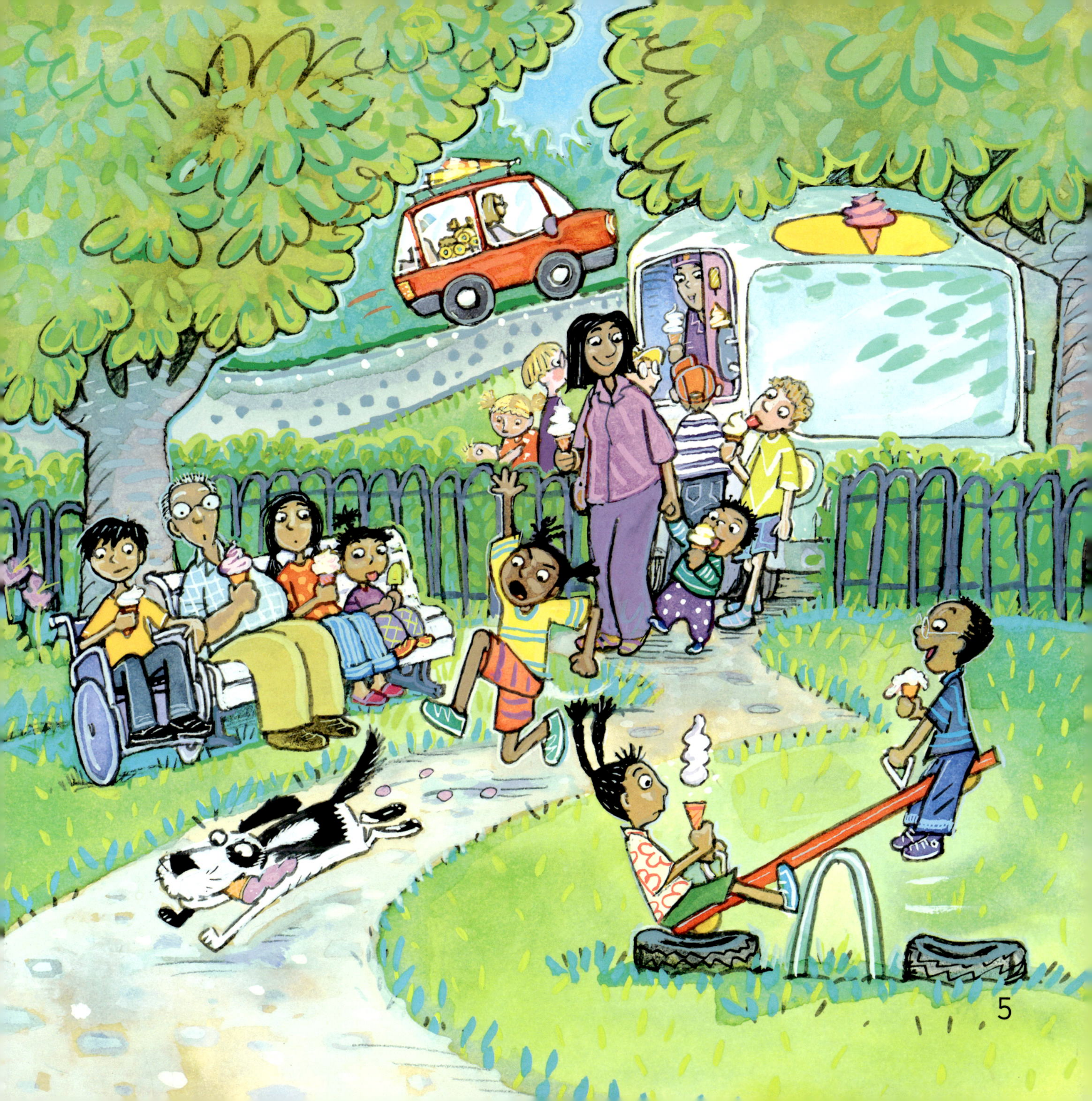

Look! We can see the sand.

7

Look! We can see the sea.

9

Look! We can see Mum and Dad.

11

Look! We can see the beach.

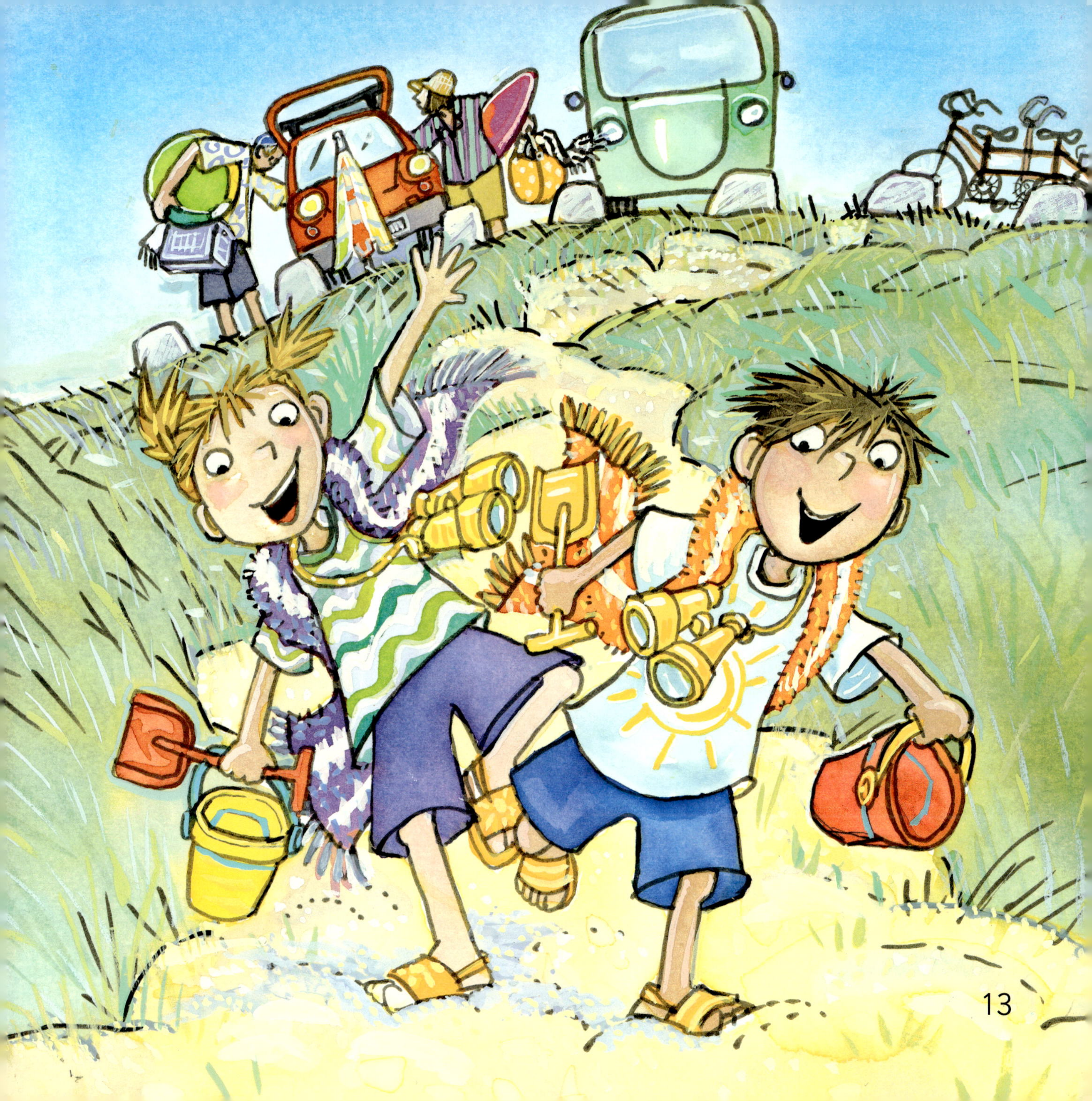

The Beach

an ice-cream van

Dad

Mum

the seagulls

the sea

the sand

Ideas for guided reading

Learning objectives: Track text in right order, page by page, left to right, top to bottom, making one-to-one matches; pay close visual attention to print, words and pictures; sustain attentive listening, responding to what they have heard; reading initial letter sounds.

Curriculum links: Knowledge and understanding of the world: similarity and differences; the features of the natural world

High frequency words: look, I, can, see, the, mum, and, dad

Interest words: seagulls, ice-cream van, sand, sea, beach, children

Getting started

- Show the children the book and ask them to point out the front cover and the title. Discuss the cover – what is happening? *Where are the family going?* Read the title together.
- Walk through the story up to p13. Ask the children what is happening on each page? Point out the binoculars. *Why do the children think they are at the beach on p2? Are they right?*
- Remind children to use pictures to help them with challenging words.

Reading and responding

- Ask the children to read independently and aloud up to p13. Observe, prompt and praise use of finger to follow text from left to right, one-to-one matching and use of picture cues to tackle difficult words.
- Model reading *Look!* with expression and discuss how the children feel in each spread (excited because they think they are at the beach; then disappointed when they realise they are not).
- Ask the children to look at the spread on pp14-15. Ask them to read each label and discuss where the children saw these things earlier in the book.